My Lamb

by
Stanley Wonderley

Illustrated by
Tiffany Jordan

INFINITY
PUBLISHING

ISBN 0-7414-6357-1

Printed in the United States of America
Published December 2010

INFINITY PUBLISHING
1094 New DeHaven Street, Suite 100
West Conshohocken, PA 19428-2713
Toll-free (877) BUY BOOK
Local Phone (610) 941-9999
Fax (610) 941-9959
Info@buybooksontheweb.com
www.buybooksontheweb.com

My Lamb

"Read to a child daily."

To: Tyler.
Read a little,
Learn a lot.
Stan

Early one March morning Dad said to me, "A baby lamb needs you." I knew just what he meant.

As I walked outside, it was just breaking day. The full moon was setting over the west hills. The wind blew the huge trees, looking like giant ghosts, in the early morning light.

I found him all alone in the pen. His mother was gone.

I gently wrapped my warm coat around his trembling body. I could feel his heart beat.

Like all animals on the ranch, I wanted him to have a name. I called him Sam.

"Now don't you feel better, Sam? I will take good care of you."

As I carried Sam into the house, my mother smiled with approval.

She knew just what to do. She got a box and a blanket. I gently put Sam in the warm box. He didn't seem to mind.

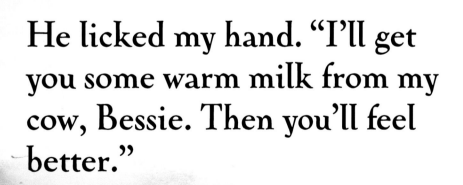

He licked my hand. "I'll get you some warm milk from my cow, Bessie. Then you'll feel better."

I went out to the barn where
Bessie, the patient cow, was waiting
for me to milk her.

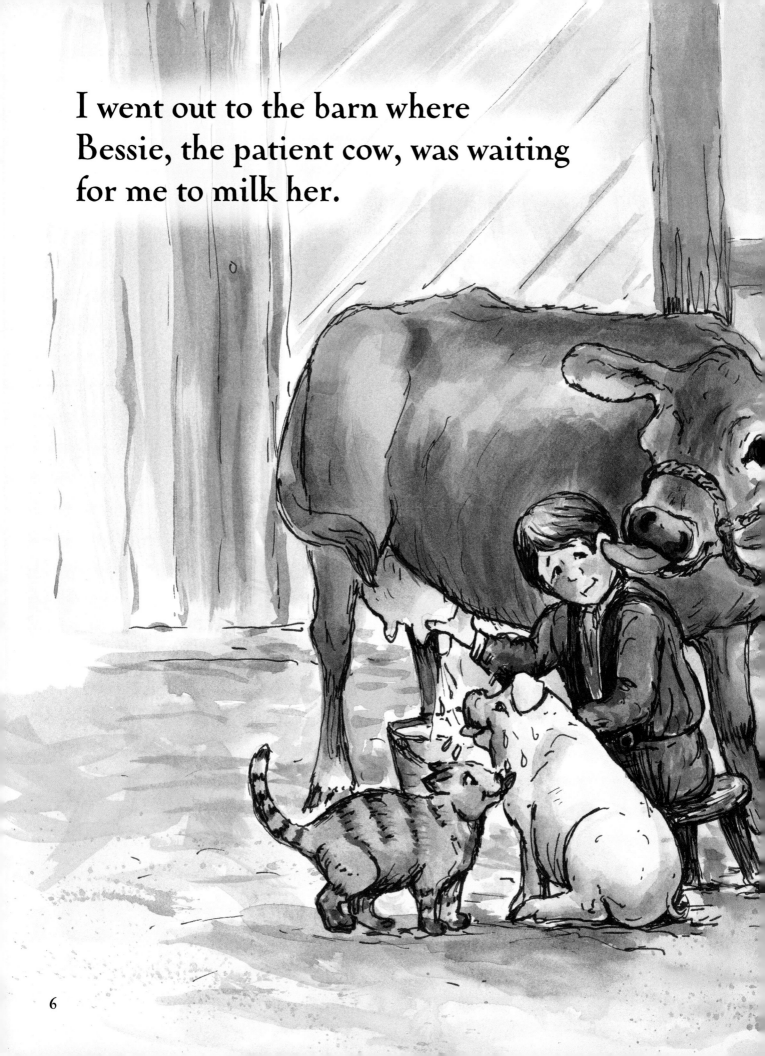

Bessie, your milk is so warm, and tasty. Sam is hungry, and your milk will be so good for him. Squirt, my pet pig, and Fluffy, my cat, love your milk."

"Bessie, you give us so much, that's why I like you," I told her as I began milking.

I brought Bessie's milk to the house. Mother soon found a bottle with a nipple that we used to feed other baby animals. She poured the rich, warm milk into the bottle. I took it to Sam.

"Sam, you will like this milk. It is from our cow Bessie."

Soon Sam stopped trembling.
"Remember, I told you I would
take good care of you," I told him.

As the months went by, Sam grew strong and healthy. When the warm spring days came in May, we took walks together.

The trees leafed out and lush green grass was everywhere. All creatures large an small were busy raising families.

"Sam, I love the spring. Everything is beautiful."

Summer came. I loved to play with Sam and our dog Shep. We were happy together. The three of us chased each other around the ranch.

Sam was growing strong,
healthy, and happy eating the
sweet green grass.

Everywhere I went, Sam and Shep
were sure to go. You are such
good friends. "I love playing with
you." Sam answered, "Ba-a-a-a-a."

It is my job to bring wood for the stove so Mother could bake some bread. Sam and Shep tagged along.

"I guess chores are just a part of life. That old cook stove sure burns lots of wood, but it's worth the work. I love mother's cooking."

One day it began to get windy. A dark cloud was coming from the north, blackening the sky.

Dad said, "It is one of those terrible dust storms. It can be bad for people and animals. Jimmy, you had better put Sam in the shed."

I gently took Sam to the shed where he would be safe. He seemed to understand. "Sam, I will take good care of you," I said.

I became worried about Sam.
He looked scared.

"Sam, don't you worry. I will take good care of you." Sam answered, "Ba-a-a-a-a." I smiled and said, "This dust storm will be over soon. Then we will play together."

I took him some water from our well. Then I got some fresh hay for him to eat.

"Sam you will be safe in this old shed. When the dust storm is over I will come and get you."

Then fall came. The days were getting cool. The leaves were turning all shades of yellow.

Sam grew big and strong. He gave me rides, and Shep led the way. When Sam ran, I held on to his soft thick wool.

We were happy playing together.

One cold winter day it snowed all day. The snow covered everything. It was beautiful.

My shoes crunched in the cold snow.
I pulled my stocking cap over my ears to keep them warm.

Sam and Shep liked the fresh white snow.
Sam had a thick coat of wool to keep him warm.

"Sam, I am glad it snowed.
It is so beautiful."

I made a sled. "Sam, I will
teach you to pull the sled,
then you can help me with my
chores."

"Ba-a-a-a-a." Sam seemed
to understand. He soon
learned to pull the sled
loaded with fire wood.

It was spring again. Sam had grown into an adult sheep. His playing was getting too rough. One day when I was in school he wanted to play with Dad.

Sam gave Dad a hard shove
with his big horns. Sam just
wanted to play. But Dad did
not think that was funny.

Dad said to me. "Sam must go. He is getting too big to play."

Our neighbor, George Johnson, wants him as a part of his flock of sheep. "You should feel very proud, Jimmy. You have raised a fine sheep."

"I know," I answered. "Lately he has started playing too rough. Shep and I are going to miss Sam. We have been such good friends."

Dad and I loaded Sam into the back of the truck. I knew Sam would be happy with another flock of sheep.

Sam was ready to go. He turned and looked at Shep and me one more time. "Ba-a-a-a-a." He seemed to understand.

We waved goodbye to the happy Sam.
"I will never forget you," I promised